CHARLOTTE'S PIGGY BANK

For Paul, Ellen and Luca

A Red Fox Book

Published by Random House Children's Books, 20 Vauxhall Bridge Road, London SW1V 2SA
A division of Random House UK Ltd
London Melbourne Sydney Auckland Johannesburg and agencies throughout the world

Copyright © 1996 by David McKee

3 5 7 9 10 8 6 4

First published in Great Britain by Andersen Press Ltd 1996

Red Fox edition 1998

Printed in Hong Kong

RANDOM HOUSE UK Limited Reg. No. 954009

ISBN 0 09 972181 3

CHARLOTTE'S PIGGY BANK
David McKee

RED FOX

One day, when they were out together, Aunt Jane bought Charlotte a present.

"Thank you, Aunt Jane," said Charlotte, as she unwrapped it. "It's, it's a pig," she said in surprise.

"It's a piggy bank - a money box," said Aunt Jane. "And this will start your savings." She put some money into the pig.

"Thank you, Aunt Jane," said Charlotte.

"Silly present," said Charlotte as she went indoors and she shook the pig to try to get the money out.

"Don't do that," said the pig. "It hurts."

"Oh! A magic pig," said Charlotte.

"Yes," said the pig. "And if you save enough you get a wish."

"Save enough?" said Charlotte. "I thought they gave
wishes away. How much must I save?"
"When you've saved enough," said the pig,
"you'll hear a 'DING!'"
"I could be saving forever," said Charlotte.
"Life can be very hard," said the pig.

"I'm saving for a wish," said Charlotte when she
was given her pocket money.
"I expect wishes are expensive," said Dad, and he
gave an extra coin.
Later, Charlotte put the money in the pig. It didn't
'DING!' and the pig didn't speak again.

"I'm saving for a wish," said Charlotte as she helped
her mum.
"That's nice, dear," said Mum and she found some
coins for Charlotte's savings.
There still wasn't a 'DING!' from the pig.

Charlotte took Mr Jack's dog for walks. She liked to help the neighbours.
"This is for being so kind," said Mr Jack as he gave Charlotte some money. Still the pig didn't 'DING!'
Mrs Adams wrote letters and Charlotte posted them.
"Here's a little something for being so helpful," said Mrs Adams. The little something didn't 'DING!' the pig either.

When Mr Grant washed his car, Charlotte helped him. They sang duets as they worked.

"That's for being so sweet," said Mr Grant, and he gave her some coins. The coins made a nice sound as they fell into the pig, but it wasn't a 'DING!'

Charlotte made a stall in the street
and sold the toys that she didn't
want any more. "You're nearly full,"
said Charlotte as she put the money
in the pig. The pig said nothing.

When Charlotte visited Aunt Jane again, Aunt Jane said, "This is for the pig," and gave Charlotte a big silver coin.
"Thank you, Aunt Jane," said Charlotte. "I'm saving for a wish."

Aunt Jane's coin did it. "DING!" went the pig.
"Hurrah, I get my wish!" shouted Charlotte.
"Yes, and I'm glad you wished that," said the pig.
"Wished what?" said Charlotte.
"You said you wished I was a flying pig," said the pig.
"I never said that," gasped Charlotte.
"You never said what?" asked the pig.

"I wish you were a flying pig,"
said Charlotte.
"That's it," said the pig and
there was a flash. There stood
the pig, only bigger and with wings.
"That's not fair, you tricked me,"
said Charlotte. "Where's my wish?
Where's my money?"

"Life can be very hard," said the pig as he flew out of the window.
"Come back," shouted Charlotte.
"Perhaps," said the pig.

Some bestselling Red Fox picture books

THE BIG ALFIE AND ANNIE ROSE STORYBOOK
by Shirley Hughes
OLD BEAR
by Jane Hissey
OI! GET OFF OUR TRAIN
by John Burningham
DON'T DO THAT!
by Tony Ross
NOT NOW, BERNARD
by David McKee
ALL JOIN IN
by Quentin Blake
THE WHALES' SONG
by Gary Blythe and Dyan Sheldon
JESUS' CHRISTMAS PARTY
by Nicholas Allan
THE PATCHWORK CAT
by Nicola Bayley and William Mayne
WILLY AND HUGH
by Anthony Browne
THE WINTER HEDGEHOG
by Ann and Reg Cartwright
A DARK, DARK TALE
by Ruth Brown
HARRY, THE DIRTY DOG
by Gene Zion and Margaret Bloy Graham
DR XARGLE'S BOOK OF EARTHLETS
by Jeanne Willis and Tony Ross
WHERE'S THE BABY?
by Pat Hutchins